For Roger

xxx

ISBN: 978-1-935021-38-4

Library of Congress Control Number: 2008935856

This edition first published in the United States 2009

by Mathew Price Limited,

5013 Golden Circle, Denton TX 76208

Manufactured in China

One Potato

Sue Porter

MP

MATHEW PRICE

"Does anyone mind if I have the last, teeny, weeny potato?" asked Goat. Everyone minded. Everyone wanted it.

"Now let's be fair," said Cow, "why don't we hold a competition for it?"

"Great!" said Goat, jumping onto his
seat. "Last one to stand on a chair, loses."

"That's going to be difficult," snapped
Cow, "since I don't have a chair."

"Such a pity," said Goat, who couldn't care less, "but somebody has to lose." Then, "The last one to stand on his head," he shouted, kicking his legs in the air.

"How can I do that?" hissed Goose,
"My neck's too wobbly."

"You've got a problem there," laughed Goat, as he disappeared up the hayloft ladder. "The last one in the hayloft loses."

"Don't start yet," puffed Pig, "I'm stuck."
"Too late old boy," said Goat, "you lose."

And with a great leap, he shouted,

"That's not fair," wailed Sheep, "I wasn't ready." And he kicked a load of hay over onto Goat.

"Perfectly fair," said Goat, "I win the
potato."

Everyone looked at the plate.

But the potato was gone!

"Delicious," said a tiny voice.

"Now children, let's tell Goat
what we had for tea." And ten tiny
mice all squeaked together,

"ONE POTATO!"

THE END

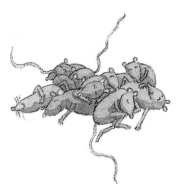